Paddington

and the Busy Day

MICHAEL BOND

Paddington

and the Busy Day

illustrated by R.W. ALLEY

HarperCollins *Children's Books*

One morning, Paddington looked out of his
bedroom window and saw that it was raining
outside.

He was very disappointed. He had planned
to spend the day in the garden and now he had
nothing to do.

"How about doing some painting?" suggested Judy. "You can borrow my box of paints if you like."

"There's a bowl of fruit in the other room," said Mrs Brown. "Why don't you try painting that?"

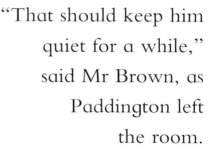

"That should keep him quiet for a while," said Mr Brown, as Paddington left the room.

But Paddington was back in no time at all. He held up the bowl of fruit for everyone to see.

"I've painted it blue so that it will match the wallpaper," he said.

"I have a feeling it is going to be one of those days," groaned Mrs Bird. "Has anyone else got any good ideas?"

"You could help Mrs Bird in the kitchen," said Mrs Brown.

"How about tidying up the loft?" said Mrs Bird hastily.

"Your stamps need putting into an album," said Jonathan.

"If you have any paste left over," said Judy, "you could stick lots of things together and make a collage like the one on the wall."

Paddington thought for
a moment.
"I think I'll start in the
kitchen," he said.
"I may make some
pastry. Bears like pastry."

"I think it's time I went to
the office," said Mr Brown.

Paddington was soon hard at work making pastry.

He used over half a bag of flour and he ended up with most of it over himself.

"You'd better go upstairs and have a wash," said Mrs Bird, "or you will end up looking like a polar bear."

"I do hope it stops raining soon," said Mrs Brown.

On his way upstairs, Paddington
remembered his stamps. His
Aunt Lucy, who lived in
the Home for Retired
Bears in Lima, was
always sending
him postcards.

He collected them all into a big pile and took
them along to the bathroom so that he could get
the stamps off with the water at the same time as
he washed.

But as soon as the water started mixing with the
flour, it turned into paste, and in no time at all
he found he had more stamps stuck to his duffle
coat than in his album.

Paddington decided
it might be a good
time to try his paw
at tidying the loft.
At least no one
would be able to
see him up there.

He made
himself some
marmalade
sandwiches and
found his torch.
Then he climbed
up the special
folding ladder
Mr Brown used for
going into the roof.

Paddington had never been in the loft before
and it was much darker than he had expected.

He hadn't gone very far when he
stepped on a loose board by
mistake.

The other end came up
and hit him on the back
of the head.

The torch went one way.
The marmalade sandwiches
went another way.
And Paddington...

...went straight through his bedroom ceiling.
Back in his room, Paddington gazed up at
the hole.

"Oh dear," he said to the world in general.
"I think I'm in trouble again!"

He looked at himself sadly in the mirror,
wondering what to do next, and as he did so he
had an idea.

   He fetched his pastry and the rest of the flour
from the kitchen. Then he collected Judy's
painting set and the rest of his stamps.
After that he found a bucket
and a large spoon
and some old
newspapers
and he set
to work.

The Browns could hardly believe their eyes
when they saw what Paddington had been
up to.

"I've never seen a collage on a ceiling before,"
said Judy.

"I wish I'd thought of it," said Jonathan.

"It looks good enough to eat," said Mrs
Brown. "Whatever gave you the idea?"

"It came to me," said Paddington vaguely.
"It's what's known
as a ceilingage.
I shall keep it
there to remind
me of all the
things you
can do on
a rainy
day."

"I think," said Mrs Bird, "rain or no rain,
it's high time you had a bath."

And even Paddington had to
agree that was the best idea
he had heard so far
that day.

"The trouble with having nothing to do," he
said, "is that you do get very sticky. Especially if
you happen to be a bear."

First published in hardback in Great Britain by HarperCollins*Publishers* in 1987
First published in paperback by Collins Picture Books in 2001
Published as part of a gift set by HarperCollins Children's Books in 2007

5 7 9 10 8 6 4

Collins Picture Books is an imprint of the Children's Division, part of HarperCollins Publishers Ltd.
HarperCollins Children's Books is a division of HarperCollins Publishers Ltd.

Text copyright © Michael Bond 1987
Illustrations copyright © R.W. Alley 1999

Visit our website at: www.harpercollins.co.uk

Printed and bound in China